THE WEIGHT OF FORGOTTEN FEATHERS

PRATHEEKSHA SUSAN JACOB

Clever Fox® PUBLISHING

Chennai • Bangalore

CLEVER FOX PUBLISHING
Chennai, India

Published by CLEVER FOX PUBLISHING 2026

ISBN: 978-93-7500-909-2

Dedication

To Ammachy, Appa, and Simba,
who live through these pages but will never read them.

FOREWORD

I wonder if everyone has experienced this feeling—whether it arrived briefly like a passing breeze or pulled us in so deeply that the world around us blurred. Love, longing, and everything in between. They find us in one way or another.

Have you ever been fascinated by the fact that some people just have a beautiful way with their words? Not just writing them, but using them to change the way you see things. I recall the first time I met Pratheeksha, level-headed and calm. The kind of person who understands more than you need to say… and yet bubbly enough to make a dull Monday meeting tolerable. She's a mentor you always wish you had and the hype person you didn't know you needed.

Like the aroma of the first brew on a slow morning, like the earthy scent before rain touches the ground. That's what knowing her feels like—cozy, warm, and soothing.

From the cup of coffee we shared to the silent walks at night, where even quiet felt like company. She makes everything beautiful and interesting.

I still remember the afternoon she asked me to write this foreword. I had a warm cup of tea in my hand, and suddenly it felt warmer. Maybe that was the excitement. You know you mean something when she trusts you with her words.

Speaking of her words, they are deep enough to make you pause mid-sentence and wonder how someone can write like this. They make you think, they make you feel, they let you experience, they fill you with warmth and excitement and a little ache, and they remind you that even the simplest moments can carry a whole lot of emotions.

This book is proof.

The Weight of Forgotten Feathers takes you on a journey through six phases of life. As you wander through the pages, you'll find yourself gently wrapped among the lines of love beautifully explained through **Love is an Unfathomable Delusion,** a piece that explores the complexities and emotional impacts of love, presenting it as an illusion that can lead to irrational behaviour and vulnerability, and **Our Book of Genesis** whispers how love fosters harmony and completeness in life.

Then comes the next chapter of life, where there is love, there is heartbreak, captured in the lines of **Lies Stuck in Your Teeth,** which revolves around themes of deception, pretence, and the performative nature of human interactions.

From here, the journey continues, now through moments heavier to bear— Death. Themes of memory, loss, and the deep emotional connection echo through **In Remembrance,** and whispers of despair and a deep yearning for renewal and growth weave through **In The Deep.**

And so the heart moves into grief, heavy yet quiet. The impact of absence, the weight of memories, and the desire to honour a loved one resonate through the lines of **Time That Bit the Dust.**

While grief lingers, the journey leads us into resilience. Where the conflict between personal identity and societal expectations is highlighted through **Condiment** and fostering connections that provide warmth and comfort amidst chaos and emotional exhaustion linger in the lines of **The Weather Inside.** As our journey continues, she invites us to her house with a choice of two rooms- Room Brain or Room Heart- and hosts us along the lines of **I Am a Gracious Host,** and the essence of embracing one's true self moves gently through **LET.**

Six phases…
Six transformations…
Sit back, breathe, and let these pages take you on a journey of the heart and mind.
I'm glad you are holding this book in your hands.

Ramyashree

ACKNOWLEDGMENT

It is easier to find and arrange the edge pieces of a jigsaw puzzle. The shape it will take is not quite a mystery. It's clear, designed, and anticipated. What comes as challenging are the remaining pieces. The process of getting those pieces in their places drains you in emotions and brings you to dilemmas. In my puzzle, these pieces induced themes of love, heartbreak, death, grief, epiphany, and resilience, just as I have felt through the journey that you now hold in your hands.

Aaliya Wahab has breathed life into my words with her beautiful illustrations and Cleverfox Publications has nursed it well to reach you.

To all the pieces, my characters who lived, loved, and left, you- I thank you. Without you, I wouldn't dare to weigh 'The Weight of Forgotten Feathers'.

CONTENTS

Love

An eternity later

Our eyes met an eternity later-
Goosebumps vined quietly like a secret.

A Glass of Fine Wine

His sweet blue eyes glimmered
In the soft hue as the candle shimmered.
Silently, I raised my glass of fine wine
Which 'gainst the candle light, glittered.

I relished the richness of the wine,
The embers burned and chilled my spine.
And a young red wine drop beaded down
The crystal, leaving a thin film, just fine.

His gaze caught my eyes shy and brown-
A gaze where you'd into oblivion, drown.
O sweet Lord! Would this be forever?
Did a handsome smile on his face crown.

"You're the finest wine I would ever want to savour
Feel every drop of you that tastes a mint flavour
With the scent of a rich ripe grape" with a slang
He said, as if doing himself a favour.

A loud merciless wind in a moment sang
In the midst. The church bell rang
Vigorously. His eyes crimson, plumed with fire
From within his smile appeared vampire fangs.

His bloodlust singed his veins with desire
My blood ripped off his patient attire.
My heart pulsed faster, deeper..impolite.
His thumb caressed my carotid in admire.

I shook awake to a moment's respite
On the coziest couch in my room so bright
"Snug as a bug in a rug" of paper crumples-
What a dream I ploughed to recite!

I sat upright, my bones cracked a couple
A slight pain resonating in my temple
And on my countertop I caught the sight of
A half filled wine glass standing all subtle.

Love is an Unfathomable Delusion

Love is an unfathomable delusion-
A beguiling assortment of passion.
I wish I had realised it
When I danced canvas
After I painted on the waltz.

Love is an unfathomable delusion-
A shy arrangement of weakness.
I wish I had realised it
When I baked coffee in the oven
And brewed a cake in the espresso machine.

Love is an unfathomable delusion-
An exaggerated stretch of infatuation.
I wish I had realised it
When I reserved a table for candlelight comedies
And booked tickets for stand-up dinners.

Love is an unfathomable delusion-
A concept construed as devotion
I wish I had realised it
When I packed to trek the oceans
And suited up to dive deep into the mountains.

Love is an unfathomable delusion-
A relentless excuse for attention.
I wish I had realised it
When I gathered rhymes to write grocery
And collected post-its to go poetry shopping.

Love is an unfathomable delusion-
An iridescent shade of affection.
I wish I had realised it
When I changed the gear of my ukulele
And tuned the strings of my car.

If only I could discern this delusion
Would I have realised this fantastical construct.
Do not judge.
I was in love.

Would you let me be your Sun?

Here's how I feel about you.
You are a beautiful mess.
When I see you,
I find someone working constantly
On themselves.
Someone passing through each phase
Over, and over, and over again
Wearing craters and freckles, dearth of life on their face-
Yet I'd keepsake pieces of you on a chain.
When I see you
I find someone falling and rising
Like the fingerpicked notes you played for me last night.
Someone who shines the brightest
When their heart is full
Until suddenly, they hide in stoic resignation.
But, O, how you wear the night on your skin
When you hide.
I admit I've been warned
I've been warned with cautionary tales
of your fickleness
When, in fact, I envy your transience
in my stillness.
When I see you,
I know I want to be with you.
I know I want to be with you
When you wear your heart on your sleeves
That you can't help but pull tides

when pain seeps through your bones.
I know I want to be with you
To pull you out from the shadows
-cause I see others lending your name for art
When they see you through their windows-
And I find no fault.
I know I glow
But I can't glow as bright as the crescent you show
And it's always a pleasure to see you grow.
Here's what I feel about you-
You'll always be my Moon.
Would you let me be your Sun?

I adore the Poet

I adore the Poet that made you-
Such symphonic poetry wrapped in an
imperfect skin.

You're beautiful

You're beautiful

Too beautiful
To fear the storms in me

Too beautiful
To smell my teen years like freshly cut wood

Too beautiful
To see me root in discontent

Too beautiful
To fluently speak silence with me

Too beautiful
To adore the dusk of my skin

Too beautiful
To bear me dissonantly cry

Too beautiful
To recite whatever I write, even when it may seem trite

Too beautiful
To worry about my premonitions when you don't have to

And I can't, to cry out loud, choose you
because you are
Too beautiful
To be the uninvited wildflower
In the garden of my heart.

A Chapter

I know I only skimmed through your chapter.
A chapter so familiar
and safe, you were.

Your paragraphs know how
I liked my coffee, how
I go dotty about men in fiction, or how
Delicately I go about my laundry.

Your lines understand how
I like my space, how
I need punctuations to breathe, or how
I choose conjunctions when I don't want to stop.

Your introduction felt like a blanket
You covered me with
When I slept on the couch
Before dog-earing your page.

Your characters valued my taste
Like how you trusted me
With your trial room selfies, or
A pink palette of lipstick shades.

Your conflict felt rather safe
Like how you noted down my Uber number, or
How you put out your hand while crossing, or
the "Text me when you reach" kind of way

Your end was crusty
Yet fleshy like the last
Slice of pizza you silently
Kept aside for me.

I apologize
I only skimmed, not read, through your chapter.
A chapter so familiar
and safe, you were.

I wonder how it feels to be your home

I wonder how it feels to be your home.
How it feels to be the fireplace
in the death of winter
Or the first sip of coffee
in the redolent petrichor of a summer.
I wonder how it feels to be that person
With whom you'd drench in the rain
and chat over a cone
Or carefully step on their prints
On the dampened sand at the beach.
I wonder how it feels to be that shoulder
You'd bury your head into
Or those that you'd choose to lie on
When a dramatic rom-com runs through.
I wonder how it feels to be your home
'cause you certainly know
How it feels to be mine.

Love story

Let me unveil another love story.
My love story is an art!
An art on a cheesy canvas
Spread on a saucy bed
Of veggies served on olive plates
And pepperoni like the blush on my cheeks.
I fell for the cheesy line in its crust.

Our Book of Genesis

Monday:
In the beginning, you found me
Formless and Desolate, a totalled wreck.
There came light when you commanded-
Evening passed and Morning came.

Tuesday:
You bent tall as a dome to show me
The limitless sky from the abyss
Of my Ocean caught in a tempest-
Evening passed and Morning came.

Wednesday:
You used your winsome faculty to show me
Fertile lands that endlessly sprout
Flowers, fantasies and sweet nothings-
Evening passed and Morning came.

Thursday:
You narrated stories and recited poems
Of how you found me twinkling from a distance.
You adored constellations over the Sun-
Evening passed and Morning came.

Friday:
And on the day of solstice, you'd known
All the birds, the caged and the gloating free,
And the sea monsters that lived within me-
Evening passed and Morning came.

Saturday:
When fall awaited winter, you'd met
All the animals that grazed me bare and
Men that immodestly gourmandized me alive-
Evening passed and Morning came.

Sunday:
And our whole universe was complete!
But we stopped creating and working
And held a feast on the day of the Sabbath-
Evening passed.

Tea and Biscuits

I wish a beating heart was easy to humble like a biscuit; the longer the biscuits are dipped in hot tea, the softer they become.

Heartbreak

I never told you where I am

I never told you where I am.
I've fallen into the same pit as you
where you fell a while ago.
When the weather was kind and tender
and look at you!
Grown bold into this exquisite tree. Almost beguiling.
Because you see, I fell now.
Right beside you; can you see me while you touch the sky?

The weather now is so uncertain-
Awfully still yet agitating.
So while I admire you
Growing out of this pit
with all the sunshine you find,
Please accept my apology.

Please know that I'm sorry to keep you waiting.
Please know that I'm sorry
that I might only grow as a weedling,
feeding off of you under your shade,
with a pinch of benign envy,
before someone roots me away from you.
Please know that I'm sorry
to keep wishing you'd wait for me.

A Mouth Full of Roses

The city lights dimmed
And stars, a billion of them,
Lit up brazen above us.
His pert little lips
Squirt roses on the phone.
Rich and sweet.
Promising and scented.
Dew drops of sweat
Beaded down my neck
In my cold room.
Secrets died and
secrets were born.
But nothing cued disguise.
Night died
and hours killed.
All that remained was
A mouth full of thorns.

Bags of Sugar

I carried your breath in my lungs
Like two bags of sugar I bought on sale.
I have kept it safe in the dark
Let alone an ant colony invade it.

I was a Stranger

I was a stranger.
A pot of ashes walking dead
On a barren ground where
Once a thought was seeded.
Stories of the genesis
Of something old were written since.
Something old, something sublime.
They called it love.

In sheer folly,
All I could see was a deceitful palette
while mastering oblivion to the monochrome.

The thought was shared
The thought was watered, and
The thought sprouted.
Rooted deep in the ground.

Daylights of promises and moonlights of passion
Let it grow wild. Wild and deep.
It grew wild and deep, bore fruits
into stories and poetry, and to think that
All of it was a Chaplin's play
Swore cede to the moment's decay.
The fruit once sweet festered within its skin
yet hung to my weight
Sans any despise.

The planted thought was a lie.
A slow, poisonous lie.

What was planted was a thought
That could rob cradles and feather beds
In return for sweet nothings and better blends.
All of it gently smothering
Through the course of seasons.

I can't breathe.
The thought must die.
I let the decay cancer it's way up
and swallow the thought so naive;
A barren land must be foreign to the green.
I let myself decay to a part of ashes.
I am now a stranger.

I Kissed You a Good Night Sleep

I kissed you a good night sleep
When you handled my trust
Like you handled your promises.

Irises that then bloomed at your grave
Now reek of your venom.

If He Asks You About Me

I may sound kind and thoughtful
to call you, but I'm tired
From carrying the burden of my intentions.
I wish you heard my pulse
Stretching the seconds by an eternity
When I longed to hear you
Speak of his name. I was deaf until then.
If he asks you about me,
Remind him not of the time
I sunk my teeth in pain.
Not of the time
I buried my head in my pillows
Listening intently to Sara Bareilles sing Gravity
Over and over for months.
Not of the time
I nurtured the art of staying blind.
Instead,
Remind him of the time
I found comfort in his chaos.
Of the time
I could read happiness from his brows.
Of the time
We didn't grow tired of sweating our palms in each other.
Because the sweetest memories
leech on you.

They suck blood out of your vein
And drift your mind from the mundane

They're vicious.
They hurt better.

Lychee

You fancy me for the ripest lychee
From the market.

If your wit wins my trust,
Break my shell
Peel off my thorns
And I'll shed my bitter skin bare
For you to taste me raw: sweet, yet
Defenceless and fragile.

I can't be the only one

I can't be the only one
searching for a map to follow.
I've been left stranded
in the middle of the woods
after I coursed through the map of your face;
Every sharp turns and bumps and folds
of your heart.
I hope I'm the only one who fell
into the pits
'cause finding my way back was perturbing.
My compass deflected
with unbridled ambition
to places where the sun set in the west.

I can't be the only one
searching for a map to follow.
I trudged the mountains
and dived deep into the oceans in yours
but barely found a valley to rest.
I've dragged myself through the forests
and walked with heavy steps on dunes
in your map
But never found a prairie for us to walk abreast.

I can't be the only one
searching for a map to follow.
Revisiting your trails in the meanwhile

may make me feel uninvited in my home.
The walls could be painted blue
and the cushion on the couch could be brand new.
My shelves could have an unfamiliar collection
beside a fresh selection of plants by the window.
The air only feels nostalgic
but not anymore like home.

I can't be the only one
searching for a map to follow.

And if you're searching for one too,
I hope you don't place the pins in my path.

A Pawn Dawns Doom

"Mom, why did Judas betray Jesus?"

One may conceive trivial
of a Pawn dressed in night
But a resilient pikeman
must always bear the shame
to protect and come true
of his King's fate.

A Fabric of your Desire

I can be a fabric of your desire
But what we weave is no embroidery.
You render me speechless and fragile as tissue
Overlooking my unbending dyneema morals.
I can sound all satin and silky for you
When I can be jute and rough as well.
I can be too cotton for you
When you don't want me to cling
But sweat a tear
And I'll hold you close and dear.
I will protect you with
My polyester will
But try wooling me out, and
I'll call out your imperial vandalism.
It would be foolhardy to
Wash your dirt and sins off of me;
I'm still going to smell like you
To dogs.
What we weave is no embroidery
But I can always be a fabric of your desire.

Charade

I hung boho tassels above my bed
To clip tiny polaroids on it.
Mirror my heart's vision as thine bred
And you make only a charade of your prosaic mind.

Tea and Biscuits

I'd rather let my tea go cold than burn my tongue; It takes courage to leave trails and milk skins rather than let it all go in steam.

Death

Dear Simba

Dear Simba,
A tree grows on you now,
the kind that bears your favorite fruit.
We know you hate the Sun. Mom and I will make sure it rains every day, just as you love.
That tree will, one day, shed leaves on you
just as you shed your hair everywhere, even on my dessert.
Don't you worry, my boy, they're going to be beautiful
just the way your hair kept me company for weeks every time I left home.

We'll make sure we leave some room on the bed.
We'll leave your favourite spot on the lawn bald.
I'll sit there every evening overlooking the gate,
waiting to greet your favorite strangers.
I may not run after them till the end of the road for you
with your goofy face
but I'll make sure they get your greetings.
I'll make sure the delivery boys continue to deliver to the "house with the golden dog."
I'll say hi to Cairo for you every day.

I'll also keep stocking up on your treats.
You'd never perform your tricks and lessons
until you see my palms clenched with them.
Dear baby, carry your lessons with you.
You know your routine: Spin, Sit, Lay, Speak, and Dishum.

Let Appacha introduce you to his people in heaven.
Let them see what a good boy you are.
Give them all a good paw with your mischievous gasps.

Those kids from the building still stand on their toes
trying to peep over the wall.
Your absence is deafening to them.
Your favorite uncles still honk in their cars at the gate
waiting for you to run to them.
Our cat?
He's been resting under the shade of this tree,
ever since,
as have you always protected him.

You despised my ukulele but adored my vocals.
I will sing 'Back Together Again'
till the world swallows me like it swallowed you.

O, to carry a heart as golden as your coat.
Your will and testament,
if you could ever prepare one with your little paws,
would carry the whole of that heart, I'm sure.

And now as you lay eternally in our garden,
Mom and I shall resort to failing
to your excellent skills to hide and to seek.
We don't miss you.
We are waiting for you to seek us.

You can rest when you're tired, my child. Rest easy.

Good night, Simba.

Love,
Chechi

The Eggs that hatched in Spring

(haiku)

Eggs hatched in the birth
of Spring; his nestlings fly high
to find their nest Bare.

In Remembrance

I remember travelling every year
with empty luggage bags
in the hopes of carrying a piece
of your kitchen when I return.

I remember how I despised the intrusion
and clapped down mosquito corpses
when Mom and I sat on the porch
to drink your tea with mangoes.

I remember running around the house
everytime you tried to get me
to wear a ridiculously white, crooked,
all-pearl necklace with a golden clasp.

I remember admiring your faculty
of having written special prayers
for every member of the family-
Both your own and the chosen.

I wasn't worried when
you peacefully took your leave-
This flight, to you,
meant going back home.

I was worried if your leave
would segue my fear
of losing a piece of myself when
your touch is left illusory.

I was worried if your silence
would invite the moment when
your face impishly evanesce from my mind-
like a rainbow that fades with time.

I was worried if your absence
would welcome a pale, hopeless void
dead and defunct to replace with another-
like life drained from a week-old rose.

I was worried if I can
ever bottle and preserve
parts of you without having to lose them-
like your scent that escapes my memory.

I would digress from my purpose
if I didn't keepsake this poem for you.
If only I can confine all of you in passages,
would I elude my fall in an endless riptide.

A Young Bride

She was a young bride,
A groomless bride in her beautiful white gown
Veiled with her mystic power of fire
Hindering an evil secret of darkness.
She chambered her power for those who used her,
She flickered under their coveted breath,
She grew worn and low in her gown,
As she dripped to their thirst.
She did not cease her flames.
She spoke with her fire till she melted
To her last.
She no longer veiled her fire whilst
Her gown trailed a mark,
A souvenir defining her mystic power
Now lost, in perpetual darkness.

A Fallen Leaf

Withered, I broke free
to return to the bosom of my mother-

A fertile grave at reception,
After seasons of recital of odes,

Now a relic of a chaotic memory,
Dumped into the past.

Slow Death

I'm happy in her arms,
Her arms clad abreast, warm
While I live in a world illegally
Claimed by the tiniest creatures.

I'm happy in her arms,
Her arms clad abreast, warm
While stepping out of the gate
Is, today, the biggest adventure.

I'm happy in her arms,
Her arms clad abreast, warmer
While I hold captive the little fresh air
Lavishly in each breath.

I'm happy in her arms,
Her arms clad abreast, even warmer
While I'm stabbed gently with
Indifference and ignorance.

I'm happy in her arms,
Her arms clad abreast, warmer than ever
While my mental labyrinth
Is the wittiest joke of all.

I'm happy in her arms,
Her arms clad abreast; Oh, she's hot,
While she gently seduces me
To her bed.

She sang her lullaby.
I was cold as ice.

Tea and Biscuits

If you find me wearing my heart on my sleeve at sunset, know I'd be as vulnerable as a tea bag in a hot cup with little sugar- Don't dunk your biscuits, I'm bitter.

Grief

Senescence

There is only as much passivity
one can feel
When you hold their hands-

All you can do
Is hope they rely on Him

All you can do
Is study every fold of their skin

All you can do
Is listen to tales every grey strand tells

All you can do
Is try to decipher the curve of their brows

All you can do
Is watch their strides grow short

All you can do
Is find a home in their matured scent

All you can do
Is throw a rictus at their senile wit

All you can do
Is stand yonder their fogging eyes

All you can do
Is carefully picture their slurred stories

All you can do
Is watch their hopes recede like their gums

The hardest thing you must do
When they selfishly grow long in the tooth
Is to confine a person, and their past
In a span of a few words on stone.

Time That Bit the Dust (Sonnet)

The clock continues to march, as it must
Marking time that we no longer share
Since when you breathed funny and bit the dust
Time has, indeed, won fair and square.

Every part of your being goes beyond compare
Even your face beneath your burial shroud.
It sings of peace and virtue and traits so rare.
Hear your pets' dirge? They'd make you proud.

Metaphorically majestic they're, you know, the clouds
They briskly assemble in heart and sky; I'm tired
The silence you left behind is viciously loud
No elegiac sympathies will get my heart less wired.

Yet I'll immortalize you, in verse and tear,
And keep your memory close, year after year.

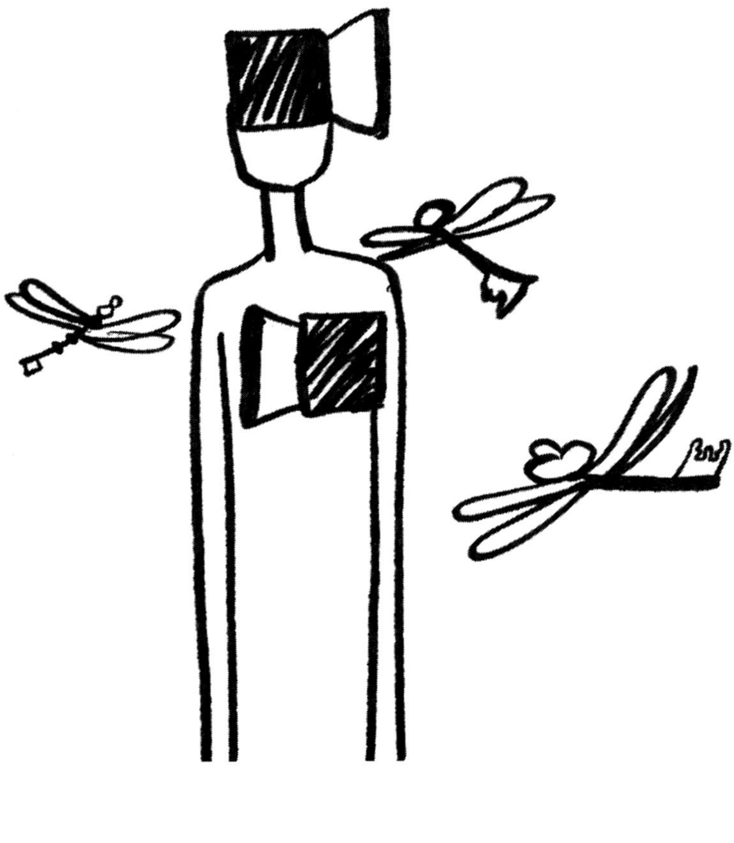

I am a Gracious Host

I am a house of two rooms-
One lit by reason, room brain,
And the other lit by love, room heart.
I'm a gracious host, but
I can't find the keys.

If I could, I would choose a room for you.
Guests come uninvited
and never leave
And they pick a room of their choice.

Things I don't wish to remember
Found room in my brain
Things I don't wish to feel
Got cozy in my heart.

I'm a gracious host
To bad memories, failures,
Arrogance and confinement
That occupied the brain.

I'm a gracious host
To grief and loss
And ruthless heartbreaks
That occupied the heart.

I'm a gracious host
but never destitute of prudence;
Residents of the brain love carefully,
Residents of the heart love harder.

I'm a gracious host
With a well-made welcome mat
and assorted refreshments
At the entrance.

You don't need a map
To find your room.
I'm a gracious host
But I still can't find my keys.

That leaves the choice to you.
Room Brain or Room Heart-
Either be a bad memory
Or someone worth my grief.

In Your Transience

Must she have borne the cross
With the passion she bore you?
For the gospels did not prepare her
For the weight through the years,
Through the cries
Through the lullabies
Through the rhymes
Through the poetry
Through the prayers
Through the final gasps
Through the silence
Through the grief.

In The Deep

I am buried deep down
Somewhere scarce in hope.

Water me with reason
So I can begin to grow again.

The Baker's Paradox

Grief: A piece of cake
No two slices are exactly the same.

Your slice may have a crown of frosting
Mine may have a crowd of chocolate chips

Your slice may have a satisfying crunch
Mine may be drooped and soggy in syrup

Your slice may be chewy, sticking to the teeth
Mine has an abandoned raisin.

We share the same flavour, yes-
But our slices narrate a different story.

Tea and Biscuits

How are you cryptic like tea?
An alchemy of a tearful of tea leaves, a soulful of milk, a drop of water, and a heartful of honey-
Yet only your leaves can manage to read, let alone break me.

Epiphany

Night is the absolute author

Night is the absolute author who can pen stories of all genres at once.

There are happy, sad, romantic, thrilling, mysterious, and overwhelming stories born every night.

When You Grow Up

They ask
"Who do you want to be
When you grow up?"
And I say,
I want to be eleven, get the Marauder's map,
solemnly swear up to no good
And manage my mischief into
Bounteous bank accounts and corporate looks.

They ask
"Who do you want to be
When you grow up?"
And I say
I want to be someone who falls terribly in love
And break my bones in the fall
So when the broken pieces heal
They mend beyond the pain.

They ask
"Who do you want to be
When you grow up?"
And I say
I wants to be anyone but a time's fool-
Ripe youth in my eyes brimming
That I can barely see my freedom and purpose
And a will that I'm forbidden to water down.

They ask
"Who are you
And what title do you bear?"
And I say
I'm someone who holds all tempests impeccably
Within the weathering ruins of my heart
For if they break and I wail with insufferable ache
I am afraid I might wake the kids.

They ask
"Who did you want to be
When you were young"
And I say
I wish I was someone
Who didn't wish to be anything at all.
All that I wanted was merely fictitious
That I did not sufficiently deserve.

I was stopped

I was stopped.
All at once.
That I was sealed with silence
To appear prissy and prim. Again.
Brick walls built around my heart
Like a fort, which,
If unrolled,
Would outdo the Wall of China.
I had unfathomable poetry,
All of 'em anything but grey,
Flooded against those walls.
I, then, went on a quest for crevices.
And I failed. Again.
And I tried. Again.
And I fell. Again.
And I still have them flooded to the cusp.
The walls have to be knocked down.
But what would the creepers
from my undone poetry cling to?

They told me to

They told me to believe in the Revelations
When I see the end getting closer-
What if I'm at the beginning of what
I deem doom in faith that falters?

They told me to bend my morals
Tenderly with kindness toward people battling a storm-
What if they were the storm
that I was battling within?

They told me to put up with the rain
To be able to see a rainbow-
What if I was caught in a riptide
when it rained?

Who'd later describe the godly rainbow
That haloed above my body;
A wreath is no more beautiful to a dead man
than the life he had spent fearing doom.

A Prism for a Pyramid

They showed me light.
Put me under an undying ray
Only to impatiently watch me grow
with a conation to refract
and discover a kaleidoscopic spectrum.

How do I tell them
they mistook me for a Prism?
Conformable and yielding.
How do I tell them
I'm, instead, a Pyramid built from stone?
Defiant and resolute.

Where in the revered scriptures
would I, perhaps, recite how
I'm home to soliloquies
Of the dead held within?

Coffee Rings

The longer you take to apologise,
The deeper is the wound intended.

The sooner you clean the coffee rings
on your table, the lighter stain it leaves.

The Weather Inside

Adulting can be despicable
When you impetuously sprout away
From your parents who tamed
All the weather inside.

There is no chilling in the swing
In the Summer of my porch
When there is dissonant Heat Waves
In my bequeathed oven.

The Tornado in the kitchen sink
Reeks worse than the aftermath
Of my clothes stuck in the Tsunami
In my broken washing machine.

Although I find comfort
In the Autumn of my study
I'm revolted at the Spring of mushroom shoots
From beneath my bathroom door.

I resort to tuned Earthquakes
On my ukulele strings
To escape the pitiful Wildfires in
The bedrooms across in the neighbourhood.

My weekends are to fix
The destructive Hailstorm in my freezer

After I clean up the Avalanche
Of milk off my bellowing stove.

I'd appreciate some warmth
To the Winter of my tired heart-
Would you like some wine
By the Volcano of my fireplace tonight?

All but a Different Story

Each of us live a different story

With the same beginning and end.

We all start from a womb,

Go through different narratives

Set lives on separate rhythms

Choose our own chronology

Focus on unintelligible themes,

Said either monotonously

Or variously adventurous,

Live them in different skins and fortune,

All of it

Only to end in a tomb

With an epitaph you'll never read.

A Broken Melody

A song sung at the summit
always has an audience.
Ready at the chorus with odious vocals
But in concert reap the experience.
For bees swarm together
When one's rich in hope and opulence
On the sweetest honey they'd feast
And speak aloud their bootless dreams.
But behold before you next strum.
There's a broken string, perhaps
Or torn cords where raspy notes break from-
The melody becomes a mere memory.
In a moment's time
When a life, mine or thine,
To grief pay gracious host,
The melody, indeed, becomes a mere memory.

With grief follows pain and a gust of wind-
Wind that winnows artless love
from sheer artful display;
To empress your barren land is now your fate.

Snowflake

A regret is a snowflake
Catch it on your tongue, and it melts.

A lifetime of them is a blizzard
There's no escape, and I'm buried to the neck.

Tea and Biscuits

Come home. I shall wait with a packet of biscuits for you to spill your tea. This time, I'll take the stain.

Resilience

A Misfit

How do I thoroughly fit in
With an undying delusion of speaking
my tongue to my foreign neighbour?
Oil and water never mix.

How do I thoroughly fit in
When my spade toils in the land
fenced beyond my sealed certificates?
I tow a trailer on a bicycle.

How do I thoroughly fit in
With princess bows and body shop hampers
in routine trash disposals and toilet scrubbings?
As useful as a sailboat on the shore.

How do I thoroughly fit in
With a will to escape estuaries
of cocktails and exhaled cancer?
A chicken perishes among wolves.

How do I thoroughly fit in
When my prized stationery and vocabulary
are now spent on weekly grocery lists?
As useful as a Cadillac on the ocean.

How do I thoroughly fit in
With a wiser stretch of skin
among assortments of imbecile brain cells?
I'm a round peg in a square hole.

How do I thoroughly fit in
When constantly melting your brain fuse
now labels you useful and worthy?
What fish out of water breathes?

How do I thoroughly fit in
With an Indian mind reciting English poetry
and a cherished Persian childhood?
I am maybe as necessary as salt in tea.

How do I thoroughly fit in
With appealing, aesthetic standards
and a bunch of funny bills?
More like louboutins that fit my package.

How do I thoroughly fit in
When I'm clearly a misfit?
Or maybe
A Misfit is someone who happens to stand out.

A Puzzle Later

And an unsolved puzzle of a reality later,
Just like that,
You were all characters
That found a place on my bookshelf.

Condiment

Time and trials revealed parts
of Lot's Wife in me-
Building home abound the people
I've known and the places visited-
Biblically branded as the
World of backsliders;
An easy ticket to perdition.
I am, now, nothing but a
relentlessly still pillar of salt-
A mere condiment to please your palate.
Dancing on a hot skillet
For the perceived defiance in my making-
What if I'd get bold
and burn your wounds instead?
Pardon me not
For adoring what I see dearly
Pardon me not
For differently interpreting divine decree
Pardon me not
For finding salvation cryptic
Pardon me not
For my disposition construed unfaithful.
I'm a Piscean
Holding an Ocean within.
I am Lot's Wife
A mere condiment.

Lies Stuck in Your Teeth

The wise father meant it when he said
"All the world's a stage."
The back stage is clogged and hideous
As the poor-graded drain.

And when the right words
went down that drain,
My notification read
"Let me make up for it."

A good, handsome couple of hours
Went for the perfect rouge and tailored fittings.
A Mary Jane strap and a backseat drive later,
The final call for the rendition was made.

There was a premium table
with wine glasses and silver cutlery
under warm, gentle lighting
In front of an instagrammable backdrop.

O men did come and men did go
With polished ties and pretentious smiles
And in every solicited visit, they served
Fine dishes that mocked my appetite.

To top it off with dessert,
In mufflements and brazen words
Of love, promises, and apologies
Was I bathed; once again.

O how beautiful are men we see
Static on stage and round in the green room!
Such performances to hold
A capricious self needs practice; lots of it.

It was my turn now-
In return for the sublime rendition
of his monologue, I gave him a toothpick;
"You got some lies stuck in your teeth."

If this world has broken you into pieces

If this world has broken you into pieces
You move on…

The shards of a broken mirror
still do it's job.

LET

Let my lungs exhale magma
Let there be spring from my eyes
Let my muffled ears blush and bruise in agony
Let light break through my crown shyness from you
Let my stretch marks grow like the whispers of the dunes
Let the ringlets of my hair tangle, or aim for the sky
Let me trace the edge of the ravine in pleasure, not pain
Let my body bear birthmarks like blots of sweet maple sap
Let the map on my palm narrate my stories
Let the celestial bed of my iris speak its truth
Let the parched riverbed of my lips know life from another
Let my brows carry all the crosses they can
Let the callus of my feet touch the abyss
Let the concave of my waist house more hugs
Let my breath burn the ground to grave my body.

When one spills poetry with her ink

When one spills poetry with her ink
All others think the sky to her is pink
Or that she inhales air to exhale stars,
Out in another world without lighting cigars

For who would blame their wits if I may ask?
With the ink of her bodkin she can immask
Anything pale with a swirl of colour
And bear a crown for her mystical valour.

She's wild when she metaphors a candle
For a ruined, shamed bride; I'll let you handle
That thought. She's a deathless roaring fire
If she can cloak a stone with magical attire.

She's no different but she thinks different
She's not loved different but she loves different
She's shown nothing different but she sees different
She is a she. That hits you different.

She may be amongst beautiful, fragile bubbles
Snug as a bug in a rug of paper crumples
With a questionable glass of rich fine wine
Spoiling her. But her magic continues to shine.

A Thank You Note

I've begun to be thankful for my skin

for wrapping around my flesh and bones,
for growing in stoic resignation,
for changing as I variously wish,
for bearing my scars,
for bleeding with me,
for tuning in after those judgements,
for not shedding away like a past,

Holding me together as a body of human meat
To feed the earth in plenty, someday.